KU-028-692

Folk Tales
from around
the world

compiled by LISA CONWAY

Ladybird Books Loughborough

A tale from Malaysia

THE ELEPHANT HAS A BET WITH THE TIGER

illustrations by **Bob Hersey**

In Kelantan there are many tales of how clever Kancil the Mouse-deer is and how, although he is as small as a cat, he manages to get himself and his friends out of many scrapes. His great rival is the Tiger and he is always pitting his wits against him.

In the beginning Gajah the Elephant and Rimau the Tiger were very close friends. But one day they met Lotong, the long-tailed monkey, who ran up a tree and sat mocking them.

"I can get him down," said the Tiger, who was very proud of his strength.

The Elephant didn't believe him and laughed, saying, "If you can get him down I'll let you eat me!"

"You try first," said the Tiger. So the Elephant trumpeted his loudest but Lotong just sat and chattered at him.

Then Rimau the Tiger crept very quietly up to the tree and everything in the jungle held its breath as he crouched and slowly swayed his tail back and forth.

Lotong became very frightened as he looked into Rimau's cold yellow eyes. Then suddenly the Tiger opened his enormous mouth and his fierce teeth shone in the sun. He roared a terrible roar and Lotong was so scared that he couldn't hold on to the tree any longer and he fell to the ground.

Rimau smiled, and turned to Gajah the Elephant and said, "Lotong may go now. I do not need to eat him because you said I could eat you and you will make a good big meal for me."

Gajah felt very frightened. He had to agree that Rimau had won the bet but he begged, "Please, don't eat me yet. Give me a week to visit my home and bid farewell to my wife and children." So the Tiger agreed and the Elephant set off home with large tears streaming down his trunk and splashing on the ground.

Friend Mouse-deer came trotting along the path and couldn't understand why the ground was so wet. "It hasn't rained for days," he said to himself — and then he saw poor Gajah plodding slowly and sadly along in front of him.

"Why, what's up with you, friend Gajah?" he asked. "Can I help you?"

"I don't think so, Mouse-deer," the Elephant said and gulped sadly as he told Kancil the sorry tale of his bet.

"Don't worry, Gajah," said Mouse-deer. "Go home to your wife and children and meet me here again in a week, but make sure you bring a jar of treacle with you."

Gajah could not imagine what Mouse-deer wanted with treacle but he did as he was told and after a week met the little deer again.

"Now pour the treacle over your back so that I can stand on your back without slipping off. Go and meet Rimau the Tiger as you promised but as soon as you see him, start trumpeting as if you are in pain."

Gajah did not think any good would come of it but he could not think of anything better to do so he set off as he was told. As soon as he saw Rimau, who was licking his lips as he came towards him, the Elephant started to crash around in the jungle as if he was in great pain. Mouse-deer stuck on his back licking the treacle so that it looked as if he was eating the poor Elephant. Then at the top of his voice Mouse-deer said, "What a shame I've only got an elephant for my supper. I wish I could find a fat old tiger to chew on."

Now as soon as Rimau heard this he turned tail and ran quickly away until he bumped into Banghor, the Old Father Ape.

"Whoa, Rimau! Where are you rushing off to so rapidly?"

Rimau described what he had seen and heard. Banghor laughed and laughed.

"I bet that's our friend Mouse-deer up to his tricks," said Banghor. "Come on, let's go back and see."

Rimau was furious that he had been tricked so he and the Ape hurried back along the path.

Mouse-deer was still on Elephant's back so he soon saw them coming and he called out, "Hullo, Father Ape. This is very bad of you! I asked you to bring me *two* tigers for supper and you've only brought me one."

Rimau stopped short and turned angrily to Father Ape, snapping at him with his shining teeth.

"You have tricked me, Banghor," he roared. "I am not going to be eaten by that terrible creature but I will eat you!"

Poor Banghor just escaped by leaping up a tree. And that is why, since then, the apes have lived in the trees, the elephant and the tiger have been great enemies and the elephant and the mouse-deer are great friends!

A tale from China

retold by **Joyce L. Pringle**
illustrations by **Valerie Sangster**

*In China, long ago, people lived very
differently from the way we do today. When a
young man wanted a wife, he did not try to find
one for himself. He would get somebody called a
go-between to find a girl for him. Even when
the go-between had found somebody whom the
young man liked, a lot more had to be done
before the wedding could take place.*

*In those far-off days, the Chinese believed
that two people could not be happy together
unless their birthdays happened to come at the
right time of the year. They even believed that
the sound of somebody's name had to be just
right.*

*If the names or the birthdays did not fit, it
did not matter how much the man and the girl
liked each other. They would never marry one
another, because they thought it would be
unlucky. Sometimes it was quite hard for a man
to find a wife at all. This is the story of one
such man...*

Long ago, in China, there lived a young man called Hsieh Tuan. His parents had died when he was a baby but a kind old friend called Mr Wang had brought him up as if he had been his own son.

When Hsieh Tuan reached the age of eighteen, he went to live in a house of his own. It was not a very big house, because Hsieh Tuan was poor, but he kept it neat and clean. He had a little piece of land nearby and there he grew rice and beans.

He did not just work in his field all day. He was also a clerk in the magistrate's court. The magistrate punished people who had done something wrong. The magistrate also listened to people who had difficult problems which they wanted him to solve. Hsieh Tuan's job was to write down the names of all these people and also everything which the magistrate had done and said. He worked very hard from early in the morning until quite late in the afternoon. Then he would go home.

He had no wife to cook for him or to clean his house, so when he reached home he had to sweep the floor and cook his own dinner. Afterwards he would go out to his field and work hard again until it was too dark for him to see.

One day Hsieh Tuan decided it was time he found himself a wife. His friend, old Mr Wang, found a good go-between. After a few days the go-between asked Hsieh Tuan if he would like to marry Miss Ch'en. She was a pretty girl who was the daughter of a farmer. Hsieh Tuan had already seen Miss Ch'en and he liked her very much. She liked him too. Unfortunately, when the go-between asked Miss Ch'en's parents when their daughter had been born, he discovered that her birthday came at a time that was unlucky for Hsieh Tuan. So Miss Ch'en could not be Hsieh Tuan's wife.

The go-between tried again and once more Hsieh Tuan was unlucky. The second girl's name had the wrong sort of sound. So it went on. Every time the go-between found a pretty girl, either her birthday or her name was wrong.

Even when Hsieh Tuan was introduced to a girl with the right birthday and the right sort of name, her parents would not let him marry her because they said he was too poor. Hsieh Tuan was very sad.

11

One night Hsieh Tuan was walking home after working in his field. He was very tired so he sat down to rest for a few minutes. The moon shone brightly and as the young man sat down he saw something by the side of the path that looked like a large, shiny stone.

He looked more closely. To his amazement, he found that what he had seen was not a stone at all. It was a huge snail.

"I am sure that this strange creature will bring me good luck," said Hsieh Tuan to himself. He picked it up very gently and carried it home with him. On the way he stopped to pick some juicy leaves for the snail to eat.

When he reached home, he put the snail in the big storage-jar that stood beside the door. He also put in the leaves that he had gathered. Then he went to bed.

When he woke up in the morning, he went straight to the jar and looked inside.

ooking my meals, then?" asked Hsieh
o is taking care of my house?"

began to tease the young man.

must have a wife after all!" she said. "I
o have one and you are hiding her! Where
g her? In a box?"

was even more puzzled now. He thanked
r seeing him and said goodbye. Then he
home. Even though he had so much to
e did not forget to take care of his snail.
ing quite fond of it and the snail seemed
g jar.

r a week, Hsieh Tuan came home to find
and his dinner cooked. He became more
ed and at last decided he must find out
so kind.

he left the house before dawn, but he
ork as usual. A little after sunrise, he
e and hid behind the fence. From here he
storage-jar just inside the door.

, he saw two lovely white hands come
. In another moment, a beautiful girl in
ped from the jar and went to the

hed into the house.

ried. "I have found out the secret!"

pale.

she said. "You should not be here.
nt to see me."

"Ah!" he cried happily. "My snail has eaten all its
leaves! It must be happy in its new home."

Before he went to work, he went out into the fields
and picked some more green, juicy leaves. He put them
in the jar and set off for the magistrate's court.

The day passed. Hsieh Tuan trudged wearily home
when his work was done. He went into his house and
stood still in amazement.

"What's this?" he exclaimed, looking round. "Who
has been here?"

On the table was a hot, tasty meal of cooked rice and
vegetables. Water had been heated for him to wash in
and the floor had been swept.

"How kind people are!" thought Hsieh Tuan. "This must be the work of good old Mrs Wang. When I have eaten this fine meal, I must go and thank her."

So instead of going to his field that evening, he called at the house of Mr and Mrs Wang. Mrs Wang was glad to see him.

"I have called to thank you for your kindness in coming to my house today," began Hsieh Tuan. "The meal was delicious."

"What are you talking about?" asked Mrs Wang. "I have not been to your house today. And what meal do you mean?"

Hsieh Tuan explained what had happened, but Mrs Wang repeated that she had no idea who had done the work for him. Certainly it had not been her. At last the young man went home, very puzzled. Before he went to bed, he made sure his snail was well and gave it some more leaves to eat.

The next day, when Hsie[h] work, he found that the sa[me] Hot water for washing sto[ne] had been swept. On the t[able] than the one that had app[eared] before. There were delici[ous] balls of fried pork, as well as the rice and vegetables.

Suddenly Hsieh pretty Miss Ch'en marry him, but p[robably] was a poor orph[an]

So after he ha[d] see Miss Ch'en. she was even m[ore] for what she ha[d]

"But I have Ch'en. "You me to do that

"Who is Tuan. "Wh[o]

Miss Ch'e[n]

"Why, yo[u] believe you d[o] are you hidin[g]

Hsieh Tuan Miss Ch'en fo[r] walked slowly think about, h[e] He was becom[ing] happy in its bi[g]

Every day f[or] the house clean and more puzz[led] who was being

One morning did not go to w[ork] crept back hom[e] could see the big

As he watched up out of the ja[r] a silken robe ste[pped] cooking pots.

Hsieh Tuan ru[shed]

"At last!" he

The girl turned

"Hsieh Tuan!" You were not mea[nt]

16

14

"But who are you?" asked the young man. "And why have you been cleaning and cooking for me?"

"Look in the jar," replied the girl.

Hsieh Tuan looked in the jar. To his surprise, he saw an empty snail shell.

"Yes," said the girl. "I came here in the form of a snail."

"Why?" asked Hsieh Tuan, very puzzled.

"I am a fairy," answered the girl, "and my name is White Wave. I was sent here to care for you because you are so good and hard-working, and because you are an orphan."

"Will you stay with me always?" asked Hsieh Tuan.

"No," replied White Wave, rather sadly. "I was meant to stay with you for ten years, until you became rich and found a wife, but now I must go. It is not proper for a mortal to see a fairy in her true shape."

"And will you ever come back?" asked Hsieh Tuan.

"No," said the fairy. "But I will leave you the snail shell. Use it for storing rice, and never empty it completely, unless bad times come. You will find it will always be full, and you will never go hungry."

As soon as White Wave had finished speaking, the sky became black. A great wind began to blow. White Wave ran across the room. When she reached the door, she spread out her arms and in a moment she was carried away in the wind. Then the storm died away.

Hsieh Tuan never forgot White Wave. He thought of her every day and always kept the snail shell. The shell was always full of rice and he was never hungry.

Before long he was made a magistrate. He was never very rich, but he always had enough. He found a good wife and they were happy all their lives.

A tale from Australia

TIDDALIK THE FLOOD-MAKER
retold by **Joyce L. Pringle**
illustrations by **Brian Price Thomas**

In the Dream Time, there lived a huge frog. He was called Tiddalik and he was the biggest frog that has ever lived. He was as big as a mountain and when he walked, he knocked down trees with his enormous webbed feet.

One morning Tiddalik woke up feeling very thirsty. He had never felt so thirsty before, and he began to drink. He drank and he drank, but still he felt thirsty.

First he drank up all the little pools in the world. Then he drank up all the lakes. Then he drank up all the streams and all the rivers. Before long, Tiddalik had drunk all the fresh water in the world. Only the salt sea was left and the animals could not drink that.

It was the dry season, when no rain falls. Plants began to die and the leaves on the trees turned brown. The animals were dying of hunger and thirst. It was a terrible time.

The animals called a meeting. Everybody came and they all began to talk about what they could do.

"Tiddalik has swallowed all the water in the world," said a bird, hopping forward. "Soon we shall all die."

"There must be some way to get the water back,"
hissed a snake. "But Tiddalik is too big and powerful to
be made to do anything he doesn't want to do."

The animals talked for a long time but they could not
think of any plan. Then at last a wise old wombat
stepped forward. "I have thought of a way," he said.
"Tiddalik must be made to laugh. If we can make him
open his mouth wide, all the water will rush out."

All the animals agreed that this was a good idea. They
went to the place where Tiddalik was resting. There he
sat, as big as a mountain, his big eyes blinking in the
sun. His body was very fat; swollen with all the water he
had swallowed.

The other animals gathered round him and began trying to make Tiddalik laugh.

"I will try first," said Kookaburra. He flew up and perched near the frog's gigantic head. He began to tell funny stories. The jokes he told were so funny that he even laughed at them himself. The other animals, even though they were so worried, laughed until tears came into their eyes.

But Tiddalik just sat there. His face did not change and his big mouth stayed shut.

The kookaburra could not make him laugh.

"Here! Let me try," shouted Kangaroo. "Come here, Emu!"

The tall emu marched up, shaking his feathers. Kangaroo suddenly jumped right over Emu. Emu walked along, shaking his head from side to side, while Kangaroo leaped backwards and forwards over the big bird. It was a very funny sight.

But Tiddalik just sat there. His face did not change and his big mouth stayed shut. Kangaroo and Emu could not make him laugh.

"That's not nearly funny enough," cried Lizard. "Watch me!"

Lizard stood up on his hind legs and began to waddle up and down. He stuck out his stomach and held out his two front legs stiffly. He looked very funny indeed.

But Tiddalik just sat there. His face did not change and his big mouth stayed shut. Lizard could not make him laugh.

Then the eel, Nabunum, wriggled towards the enormous frog. Nabunum usually lived in rivers and streams but they were all dry now and so he had been driven out onto the land to try to find more water.

Nabunum stood up on end and began to dance.
Slowly at first, he twisted and turned, bending his body
into strange shapes. Then he began to dance faster and
faster, twisting himself into every comical shape he could
think of.

Tiddalik's eyes lit up with amusement. Suddenly he
opened his huge mouth and laughed loudly.

All the water he had swallowed gushed out in a great
flood. The earth was covered with water. The ponds, the
lakes, the streams and the rivers were all filled. The
plants began to grow again and green leaves appeared.
The world was saved.

A tale from Guyana

BABY FISH

retold by **Grace Olney Nichols**
illustrations by **Brian Price Thomas**

Baby Fish lived with his mother in a green nest far below a river. The river was warm and clear and wavy. Baby Fish and Mother Fish spent many happy days darting between the waves and swimming down and down to their little nest on the bed of the river.

Mother Fish was very fussy about Baby Fish because he was her only child. She never let him out of her sight as she feared he might come to some harm. Baby Fish was a real busybody and could not stay still for a minute. He teased the other fishes by pulling their tails. Sometimes he hid among the weeds and rocks while his mother looked high and low for him. Baby Fish had bright sparkling eyes, tiny scales of gold and black and a tail that switched merrily as he moved.

One day Mother Fish felt that it was time Baby Fish learnt something about the world. So she took him right to the top of the shining river. There she showed him the bright sunshine and green grass that grew on the earth above. Baby Fish was so thrilled that he gulped and gulped with astonishment at what he saw.

Next Mother Fish took him a little farther down in the water and said, "You have seen how lovely the world can be. Now, let me show you how cruel it can be also."

Baby Fish wondered what his mother meant. Suddenly she stopped and pointed to something small and red, wriggling in the water.

"Do you see that?" she whispered.

"Yes," said Baby Fish, wondering what it was.

"That is called a worm," said Mother Fish. "It looks nice and juicy, but there's a sharp hook inside waiting to catch us fishes."

"How?" asked Baby Fish with eyes wide open.

"Well," said Mother Fish, "if you or me, or any other fish, should bite at that worm, the sharp hook inside will hook us by the mouth and we will be pulled right out of this warm river."

"And what will happen then?" asked Baby Fish.

"Some fisherman will take you home, cut you open with a sharp knife, then fry you and eat you."

"How dreadful!" gasped Baby Fish.

"Yes," said Mother Fish sadly. "That is the end for most fishes." And she turned to Baby Fish and looked him straight in the eye, "Promise me that you will never go near such a thing, Baby Fish," she said.

Baby Fish gulped and promised to do as he was told.

Well, as time went by Baby Fish began to grow a bit bigger. His mother would now let him swim around their nest all by himself but she always warned him not to go too far away. But a day came when Baby Fish felt tired of swimming round and round the little green nest. He wanted to see something else.

"What harm can there be in going off for a while?" he thought. "I'll be back before Mother even wakes up." So with a thrill in his heart and a switch of his tail Baby Fish headed upwards into the clear wavy water.

"What fun this is," he said to himself, as he passed a small grey terrapin and a snail. He flicked his tail at them then turned on his back for a swim. Never before had he had such fun. He darted, he glided, he whirled.

All of a sudden Baby Fish saw a little red thing hanging at the end of a string in the water. It was the same thing his mother had shown him.

"My goodness me, a worm!" he gulped and darted back in fright. And sure enough it was. But the worm looked so soft and juicy that Baby Fish wondered if a sharp hook really was inside.

After staring at the worm and wondering for some time, Baby Fish felt that there was no harm in touching it with his tail, simply to find out if it was as soft as it looked.

Baby Fish could not imagine a sharp hook inside. But he wanted to be quite certain. He swam around the worm, then quickly touched it with his tail. The red juicy worm wriggled slightly. It felt very soft.

But Baby Fish wanted to be quite, quite certain that there was no hook inside the red worm, and the only way he could do this was by taking a nip at it.

And that was just what Baby Fish decided to do.

"Only a little nip, only a little nip, then I'll know for sure," he told himself, as he moved closer and closer to the worm.

The next moment he opened his mouth and took a bite. As soon as he did this he felt a hot pain running through him. The sharp hook had caught Baby Fish.

Up and up he went, until all of a sudden he was out of the river and into a world of brilliant sunshine.

The sunshine dazzled his eyes. In a daze he saw that he was hanging from the end of a long rod. A big fisherman standing on the green shore had the rod in his hand. The big fisherman pulled in the rod, unhooked Baby Fish and threw him on the warm dry grass.

Baby Fish flapped for all he was worth, but all he could feel was the grass and the hard earth beneath him. With a sob he remembered all that his mother had told him.

Suddenly, Baby Fish felt a big hand curl around him.

"Oh!" he thought. "This is the end."

But the next moment Baby Fish was flying through the air and landing with a small plop back in the river. "You're much too small to be eaten," said the big fisherman, as he threw him back. "But the next time I shan't spare you."

In the meantime Mother Fish had woken up and was frantic with worry. She was looking high and low for Baby Fish. Among the rocks, among the weeds, among the shells. Baby Fish was nowhere in sight. Mother Fish was wondering where else to look when suddenly she heard a gulp behind her, and turning her head sharply she saw that it was Baby Fish. The corner of his mouth was bleeding and a tiny silver tear dropped from his shining eye.

Mother Fish did not have to say a word. She knew just what had happened. She knew that Baby Fish had learned his lesson, so very slowly, the two swam down to their nest.

A tale from Italy

BEPPO AND THE ORANGES

retold by **Dorothy Aitchison**
illustrations by **Linda Worrall**

Once in Italy, there lived a young Prince called Beppo.
He used to dream that one day he would marry a girl
with hair as gold as orange peel, skin as white as orange
blossom and a temper as sweet as orange juice.

One day he decided that he would go and find her, so
he put on his cloak, packed up some food, and set out.
He was walking along a country road when he heard
groans coming from behind a hedge. He went over and
saw a leg sticking out of the bushes.

"Hold on," he said. "I'll help you."

He pulled hard and found that he was dragging an old tramp from the undergrowth.

"Thank you," said the tramp. "I was very uncomfortable."

"Poor man," said Beppo. "Take my cloak. You look hungry, too. Have some of my food." When the tramp had eaten, he asked Beppo where he was going.

"Oh," said Beppo, "I'm off to find a girl with hair as gold as orange peel, and skin like orange blossom."

"Well," said the tramp, "before you find her you will have to pass some witches along the road. Take some twigs. The witches have an oven, and they will want to clean it."

"Yes, I'll do that," said Beppo, and he took a handful of twigs and went on his way.

Sure enough, he came to a hut and peeping inside he saw an old oven. Three witches stood nearby.

"Good day, old ladies," said Beppo. "I've brought you some twigs to clean your oven."

"Tee-hee! Thank you," cackled the old witches. "And where are you off to?" Beppo told them that he was looking for a beautiful girl with hair as gold as orange peel.

"Tee-hee!" giggled the witches. "Before you do that you will have to pass three hungry dogs. Take this loaf of bread and feed them. Then you will be able to go by!"

Beppo continued on his way. Just as the witches had foretold, he came to a narrow path guarded by three fierce dogs who growled and snapped as he approached. Beppo was ready for them.

"I hear you like bread," he said, and he tore up the loaf and threw it to the snarling animals. When they had gobbled up the bread the dogs were more friendly. "Not many people come this way," the biggest dog said. "Where are you going?"

"I want to find a beautiful maiden, with hair as gold as orange peel."

The dogs nodded their heads wisely. "To reach her, you must go through a rusty gate. Take this oil-can and you will be able to open it," said the dogs.

"I'll remember," said Beppo, and said goodbye.

Beppo travelled along the narrow path until he came to the rusty gate. It stood in front of a high tower. He pushed it but it would not open, so he took out the oil-can and oiled the hinges.

"That's better," squeaked the gate. "What do you want here?"

"I'm looking for a beautiful wife with golden hair, and skin like orange blossom," said Beppo.

"You'd better climb the tower and take three oranges then," said the gate. "But be careful, an old woman lives there and her son is an ogre!"

"I'll take care," said Beppo and ran up the stairs. The oranges were on a shelf but just as he reached for them an old woman appeared.

"My son is coming," she quavered. "He'll eat you up, for sure!"

With that, there was a terrible roaring noise and a great ogre appeared in the doorway. "I'll have *you* for supper," he shouted.

"No, you won't," said Beppo and, seizing the oranges, he hurried down the stairs. Panting and

roaring, the ogre clambered down after him.

"Stop him!" he yelled to the gate.

"Not I," said the gate. "He oiled my hinges!" Beppo ran down the path pursued by the ferocious giant.

"Seize him!" roared the ogre, as Beppo scampered past the dogs.

"No," said the dogs. "He fed us. You never did." Beppo rushed past the witches' hut. The giant had nearly caught him by now.

"Trip up that boy!" ordered the ogre.

"Never!" screeched the old witches. "He was kind to us. When have you been kind?" Beppo ran on and on, and at last the wicked ogre gave up the chase.

The Prince was quite exhausted and very thirsty. There was no water nearby and he lay panting and

breathless. Suddenly, he remembered his oranges. Beppo took one from his pocket and was just going to bite it when it mysteriously rolled away. Then he picked up the second orange. He was about to bite this one when it changed into a beautiful maiden with golden hair and a milk-white skin. "Give me some water," she pleaded. Beppo had no water, and slowly the girl disappeared.

Still tired and thirsty, Beppo stumbled on, until at last he came to a little waterfall. He sat down on a grassy bank. As he did so, he realised that he still had the third orange. He took a bite at the peel and it turned into a lovely girl. Her hair was as golden as the orange peel, her skin was as white as orange blossom.

"I am so thirsty," she said, sadly. But this time Beppo fetched her some water.

"I think you have been looking for me," she said. Beppo had at last found the girl he was seeking.

THE SPIDER AND THE ANTELOPE

illustrations by **John Flynn**

Two men called "Good-is-never-lost" and "Evil-is-never-lost" went to make a farm. They chose a good place and began to cut the trees, but did not clear the bush. When this was done they waited at home till the dry season should come. This would allow them to burn the bush before they dug the ground.

It happened that Spider, ignorant of the danger, began to spin his web there, and he married and had a large family. Antelope also came and said that it was a good place to live, cool and fertile, with plenty of fresh leaves.

Both Antelope and Spider lived there in peace and contentment without fearing anything in the future. But soon "Good-is-never-lost" and "Evil-is-never-lost" came to burn the bush. They brought confusion where there was peace before.

Antelope jumped up hurriedly to leave the bush, but Spider said, "Stop."

He said to him, "Alas! Antelope, if you do not help me and my children, how shall we escape from this danger?" But Antelope did not choose to listen for he wanted to escape alone. Spider continued to beg him; promising to repay the debt. Then Antelope asked him, saying, "How can you, who are only a spider, help me? I am strong and can run swiftly."

Spider continued to beg him, and eventually Antelope

40

agreed. He lowered his head to the ground and Spider, with his family, climbed on his back. Antelope then rushed away. When he had left behind the heat of the fire, which was great, he lowered his head again. Then Spider and all his children climbed down and they thanked him.

The place where they went to live was near a path leading to a village. The law of the animals was that they should not plant their feet in the middle of the path and leave footprints because of the hunter who used to hunt there. But Antelope forgot and crossed that path one day when the rain that had fallen had not dried up.

Antelope had not long passed when a hunter came by. He looked on the ground and saw the prints that Antelope had made. The hunter ran home quickly to fetch his gun. He also told all his friends that he was going to kill Antelope, whose foot-marks he had seen on the path.

When Antelope saw what the hunter was doing he ran to Spider to ask him what he should do. Spider then brought all his family to that path and they spun their webs so that they covered up all Antelope's tracks completely.

The hunter brought all his friends there but they saw
no marks of Antelope, for Spider had covered them.
The other hunters began to mock him, saying, "Truly
you are a fool. You see that a spider has covered the
thing, yet you can say that Antelope has passed today."
They cursed him greatly and he went home angry, while
they followed behind him.

Antelope went to Spider and thanked him because he
had saved him from death.

A tale from Canada

WESAKEJAK MAKES THE NEW WORLD

retold by **Lyn Harrington**
illustrations by **Brian Price Thomas**

A long time ago, the rains poured down and the rivers
and lakes spilled over their banks. A Great Flood
covered the earth.

Wesakejak, the big brother of birds and animals,
made a large raft, and rescued some of the creatures.
There was Otter, Beaver, Muskrat, Turtle, Caribou,
Bear, Wolf, Raven and many more, including Man. But
the raft was not big enough to hold every animal and
bird and insect, and so, many forms of life perished.

The seas rose and flooded inland. They rose until they covered the highest mountains, and no land could be seen in any direction.

After many days, the water stopped rising, but the land did not re-appear.

Wesakejak said, "If I had a little bit of earth, I could make a new world, one big enough for everyone." He could not *create* even a grain of sand, but he could change the shape of anything. He called Otter over to him, at the edge of the raft.

"Brother Otter, you are strong and brave and a good swimmer." Wesakejak knew how to flatter. "Dive to the bottom and bring me some mud."

Otter slid smoothly over the side of the raft. Little bubbles of air streamed up as he went down. After a while, he came up gasping for breath. The water was so deep he had not even seen the bottom.

Wesakejak called Beaver over to him.

"Brother Beaver, you are strong, brave and a wonderful swimmer. Bring me up a handful of mud, and you can have a snug lodge of mud and sticks in my new world."

Smack! Beaver slapped the surface of the water with his flat tail before he dived. Down he went, and down. He was gone a long time. But he came up without having touched the bottom.

"Try again!" Wesakejak shouted. "Try harder. I will make you a wife to live in your lodge."

That made Beaver try very hard. Down, down, down he swam with his webbed feet. He was near enough to smell the ground, but he could not reach it. Nearly dead, Beaver floated up to the surface.

Now Wesakejak called Muskrat over to him.

"Brother Muskrat, you are small but very brave, and you are a good swimmer. Bring me up even one grain of sand and I will make a new earth for all of us. You may have first choice of where you will live."

46

Muskrat thought for a while before answering.

Then Wesakejak promised, "I will make roots for you to eat, and will give you many children."

"Then I will try," Muskrat squeaked. "But tie something to my tail to pull me up in case I die."

Wesakejak took a piece of rawhide and cut it into a string – long, long, long – and tied it to Muskrat's tail. He promised to pull him back to the raft.

Ch'muck! Muskrat dived straight down, using his skinny tail for a rudder. Down, down, down... He was dying for lack of air. One claw scraped on mud before he sank dead to the muddy bottom.

The rawhide line went slack. This showed Wesakejak that Muskrat had touched bottom. He pulled in the line. Up came Muskrat, his little arms crossed over his chest, with mud in one claw.

Wesakejak wasted no time. Quickly he took up his long hollow reed, and blew into Muskrat's nostrils. This brought him back to life. Soon the little creature was breathing again, and boasting of his adventure.

Wesakejak put the tiny bit of mud to dry on Turtle's hard back. Again he blew, gently at first, then harder and harder.

The mud turned into dust, and grew and grew. And as it grew, Beaver flattened it out with his tail to make a large island. At last the island was so big the creatures could not see where it met the water.

Now Wesakejak rested. "My new earth has to be big enough so that every creature can have a place of his own. Brother Caribou, you are a strong runner. See if you can run to the edge of my new world."

Caribou went off at a gallop, his ankles clicking. He came back at sunset. "No, your world is not big enough for all these creatures."

Wesakejak
blew some more.
Now he needed Bear to
flatten out the heaps of
earth. But Bear was
so heavy that water
oozed up in his footsteps.

"I shall call these
swampy places 'muskeg'
after you, Muskwa the Bear."

The earth must surely be big
enough now, Wesakejak thought.

"Brother Wolf, you are a
swift runner. Run around my new
world and see if it will hold everybody."

Wolf returned in two days' time.
"It is very big, almost big enough."

49

Wesakejak blew some more, and this time he sent out Raven. He knew Raven loved the empty spaces. And when he did not come back, Wesakejak knew the earth was the right size.

He sat down by his campfire and began to give each creature its own special place, one it would like best. Otter, Beaver and Muskrat could live both on land and water from now on.

Muskrat had first choice, of course. He chose the Great Water for his kingdom.

Then Wesakejak grew forests and grasslands full of food. Muskrat thought he had made a mistake. He decided he would prefer to live on the grassy shores.

Wesakejak agreed. But when the land dried out and the hills were formed, Muskrat was not sure he had chosen wisely. He wanted to change his mind once more.

That made Wesakejak cross. "One minute you want the Dry Places. The next minute you want the Wet Places. I will give you a kingdom that is half land, half water."

Muskrat was happy with a marsh of rich green grasses and deep water. *Ch'muck*! He dived down among the roots and rushes.

He always had plenty to eat, as Wesakejak had promised. And he had many, many children; for without Muskrat, Wesakejak could not have made his new world.

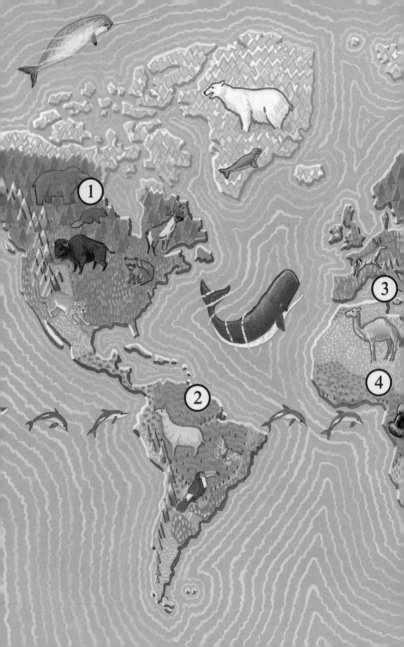